GO AWAY, WORRY MONSTER!

For Charlotte. Heartfelt thanks to Narelle and Danielle.
– B.G.

For Monte, with enormous thanks and love.
– R. T-L.

First published 2020

EK Books
an imprint of Exisle Publishing Pty Ltd
PO Box 864, Chatswood, NSW 2057, Australia
226 High Street, Dunedin, 9016, New Zealand
www.ekbooks.org

A CiP record for this book is available from the National Library of Australia.

ISBN 978-1-925820-39-3

Designed by Mark Thacker
Typeset in Minya Nouvelle regular 15 on 25pt
Printed in China

This book uses paper sourced under ISO 14001 guidelines from well-
managed forests and other controlled sources.

10 9 8 7 6 5 4 3 2 1

GO AWAY, WORRY MONSTER!

Brooke Graham & Robin Tatlow-Lord

Late one night, Worry Monster
climbed into Archie's bed.

'Please go away,' begged Archie.

Worry Monster sprang off the bed.

'How can I leave you alone when you're
starting a new school tomorrow?
There are so many buildings.
You could get lost!'

Archie's head throbbed.

'What if I can't find
my classroom?' He hugged
Brown Teddy.

'Your new teacher will probably make the class do Maths all day long,' Worry Monster whined.

Archie's tummy fluttered.

'What if we don't get to play sports?'
He checked that Toby was still curled
up beside him.

'The kids might not include
you in their games.'
Worry Monster bit his claws.

Archie's heart pounded. 'What if I don't make friends?'

He pulled Owl closer.

Archie longed to climb into bed
with his parents. Worry Monster
was scared of them, and would
quickly leave.

But Archie was a big boy
now and he thought
it was time to handle
Worry Monster by himself.

Archie remembered how he and his mother
made Worry Monster go away last time.
He could follow the same steps now. But he
was afraid that they had only worked because
Worry Monster was scared of Mama.

Archie decided to give them a try. If they didn't work, he would go to Mama.

First, he took a few deep breaths.

The air in his lungs made his belly grow bigger like a balloon.

Then Archie thought of the facts.

'FACT ONE: I can't get lost
because my new school only
has five classrooms.'

Archie folded his arms and scowled
at Worry Monster.

'FACT TWO: My new teacher does let the children play sport. The timetable says sport is every Friday afternoon.'

Archie puffed out his chest and lifted his chin.

'You won't make friends,' said
Worry Monster, wringing his paws.

'FACT THREE: I already know two boys in my class from soccer club.'

Archie pointed to his bedroom door.

'Go away,
Worry
Monster!'

Archie realized proudly that he'd almost made Worry Monster go away all by himself!

All he had to do now was ignore Worry Monster.

He wriggled closer to Owl
and looked at the pictures
in his favourite book.

'PLEASE don't ignore me!'
wailed Worry Monster.

But that was exactly what Archie did!

Turning the last page of his book, Archie
realized Worry Monster had gone. His head
didn't throb, his tummy didn't flutter,
and his heart wasn't pounding.

'I made Worry Monster go away all by myself!'

Archie stroked Toby.
'I can handle school by myself too.
I can't wait for tomorrow!'

He dimmed Owl's glow.

Archie cuddled Brown Teddy
and rolled over to go to sleep.